FOX and the FIRE

FOX and

Illustrated by John Schoenherr

the FIRE

by MISKA MILES

An Atlantic Monthly Press Book

LITTLE, BROWN AND COMPANY   Boston   Toronto

LIBRARY OF CONGRESS CATALOG CARD NO. 66-10820

Third Printing

ATLANTIC-LITTLE, BROWN BOOKS

ARE PUBLISHED BY

LITTLE, BROWN AND COMPANY

IN ASSOCIATION WITH

THE ATLANTIC MONTHLY PRESS

Published simultaneously in Canada
by Little, Brown & Company (Canada) Limited

PRINTED IN THE UNITED STATES OF AMERICA

For Emilie McLeod

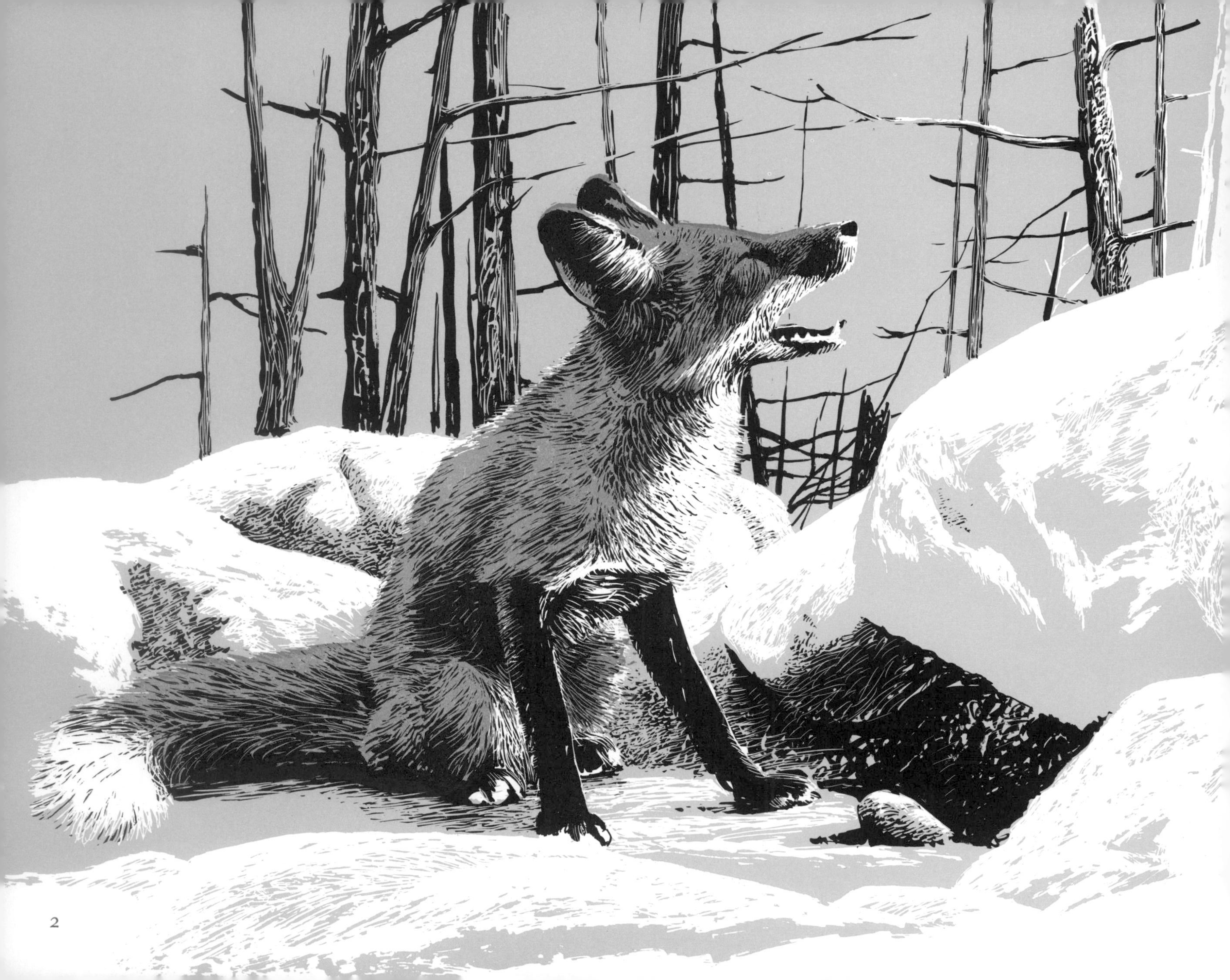

The young red fox pointed his nose toward the forest and barked quickly and sharply.

He knew the ways of the sweet, green forest. He knew where to find the rabbit and the squirrel, the possum and the weasel.

Now he stood near the entrance to his cave on the side of a mountain near the forest.

Alert he waited.

For three days, a strange, strong scent of danger had come with the wind.

Now, with the scent of danger, came the familiar and good smell of rabbit.

And the young red fox was hungry.

Cautiously, he started out to catch his supper.
He made no noise.
Near a wild lilac bush, a gentle rabbit nibbled a weed.
The fox saw him and crept close.

Before the fox could seize his supper, a bluejay darted low and screeched his anger, and the rabbit flashed into its burrow.

6

The fox whimpered and sniffed at the entrance of the burrow and scratched at the earth.

Even as he whimpered, gray-black smoke came heavy on the wind. In the distance, fire crawled along the ground and fallen leaves snapped and crackled in its path. He heard the roar of flames leaping from one madrone tree to another, and he knew he must run.

At first, he was bewildered and he did not know which way to go.

Rabbits and mice came from their hiding places.

Squirrels darted along the ground, and quail called
alarm from the greasewood.

The fox shook with a strange new feeling of fear.

Two chipmunks scurried past, and the fox followed
close behind them.

Sparrows and bluejays, starlings and flickers flew low overhead as the crackle of fire came closer.

Together the animals ran out of the forest, and the fox forgot his hunger.

On they went, across green fields, through a walnut grove, and between rows of grapevines growing on the mountainside, until they came to a road.

The fox followed beside the road, and he was half hidden in the tangle of brush that grew near a fence.

He came to a low brown house with a fig tree growing beside it.

Beyond the fig tree was a barn, red-black in the fireglow. Between the barn and the house was a pen, and inside the pen a small chickenhouse.

With the strong, close smell of chicken came the smell of enemy. The fox shivered in terror. For a moment, he flattened himself against the earth.

In the flickering shadows of the tree, a man with a hose in his hand directed water to the roof of the ranchhouse.

The fox crouched, tense, ready to run, but there was no place to go.

In the distance, the fire approached the vineyards and flamed up and died back at the edge of the cultivated earth. But it burned like a furnace in the walnut grove, and it crawled slowly and angrily along the side of the road, now smoldering, now flaring up and burning brightly again.

Inside the house, a dog barked wildly, and the fox ran to the barn, hunting around it for a place to hide. Beneath the barn, he found a small opening into which he crawled. He lay there, his nose on his paws, watching...

Rabbits and chipmunks, squirrels and mice found hiding places; squirrels and chipmunks in the fig tree, rabbits and mice under the house.

Raccoons came and found shelter.

Five deer came, timid, watchful, and lay down close beside the barn.

The fox felt the rumbling of the earth when the fire-trucks rolled up, their red lights flashing and their sirens screaming.

Cars came, and men climbed out to help fight the fire. With shovels and spades they turned the earth. With wet burlap sacks they struck at the fire.

Tanker trucks filled with water arrived, and a firefighting bomber flew low overhead.

Bulldozers scraped the earth to hold back the fire. Sparks flew through the air, and those that found the wet roofs and the turned earth sputtered and died.

Inside the house, the dog howled long and mournfully, like a wild animal.

In the hours that followed, the fox huddled small in his shelter, his heart pounding hard against his ribs.

The people at the ranch fought the fire with the firefighters, and the fire was held back along the ground by the freshly turned earth. The house and the buildings, the fig tree and much of the vineyard were saved.

When the fire was out, the men went inside the house, and the fox remembered that he was hungry.

He crept outside and cautiously, fearfully, he approached the house.

Inside, beyond the window, he saw a fat white cat stretched out on a red chair, and a big black dog pacing back and forth, back and forth, whining deep in his throat.

The fox pointed his nose toward the forest.

Only the ugly, charred smell of burned wood came with the wind.

Trembling, with his belly close to the ground, he crawled toward the road.

He crossed into the vineyard. Afraid, he crouched there between the rows of grapevines, waiting until he could return to his cave.

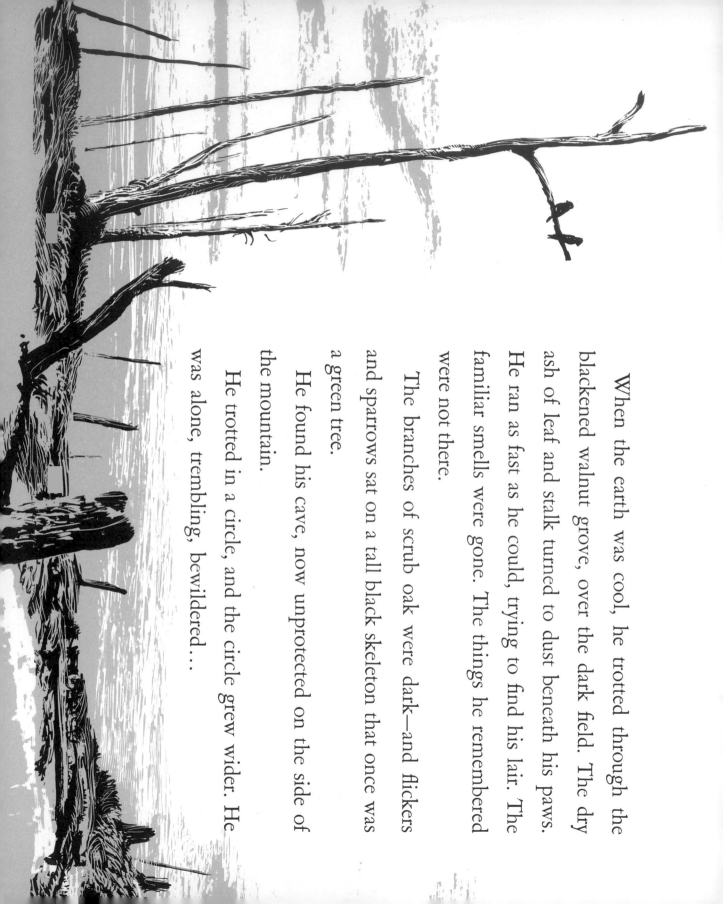

When the earth was cool, he trotted through the blackened walnut grove, over the dark field. The dry ash of leaf and stalk turned to dust beneath his paws. He ran as fast as he could, trying to find his lair. The familiar smells were gone. The things he remembered were not there.

The branches of scrub oak were dark—and flickers and sparrows sat on a tall black skeleton that once was a green tree.

He found his cave, now unprotected on the side of the mountain.

He trotted in a circle, and the circle grew wider. He was alone, trembling, bewildered...

He hunted for his breakfast, but the rabbits and the mice had gone to new hiding places and the fox found nothing.

He hunted all day, and when night came, he started out across the black pastures and the walnut grove. He

followed along near the charred fence beside the road.

He pointed his nose toward the wind, and the smell of chicken came strong and clear, and his stomach grew tight with hunger.

When he reached the ranch where he had found
shelter, he crept to the barn and crouched there, waiting, listening, sniffing the air....

He smelled dog and man.

But there was no sound from the low brown house.

Cautiously, he crawled toward the chickenhouse.

With a mighty leap, the thin, hungry fox scrambled
over the fence.

Without making a sound, he crept inside the chickenhouse.

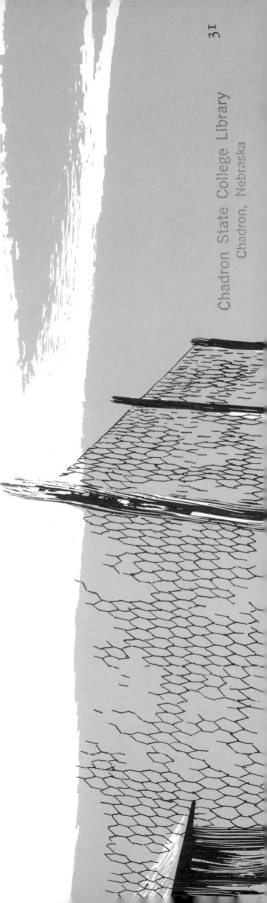

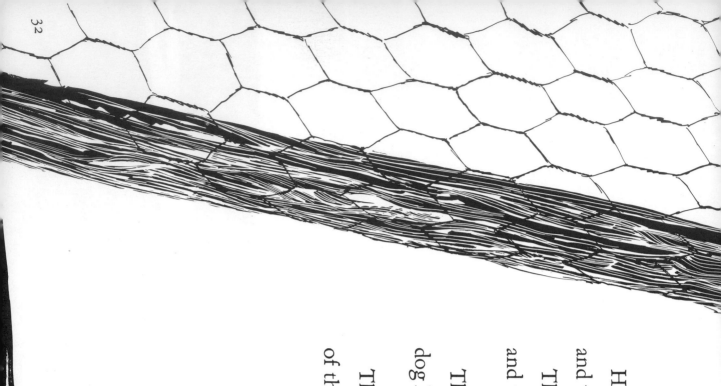

He reached up and seized a chicken from its perch, and with one quick shake of his head, it was dead.

The chickens roosting there set up a great squawking, and the fox sprang up and over the fence, and away.

The door to the house opened. People shouted. The dog leaped from the doorway, yelping in his excitement.

The fox ran straight toward the road. The shrill bark of the dog was closer—closer...

The fox galloped along beside the fence. He crashed under a clump of blackened brush and leaped to the top rail of the fence.

The dog went racing past.

The fox went on along the fence. The charred wood crumbled between his toes. He jumped down and raced lightly through the vineyard.

Now, far in the distance, he could hear the unhappy yelps of the dog.

Then there was silence.

Back in the barnyard, the dog trotted up, panting loudly, and the chickens scolded softly and settled down again to sleep.

The fox did not return.

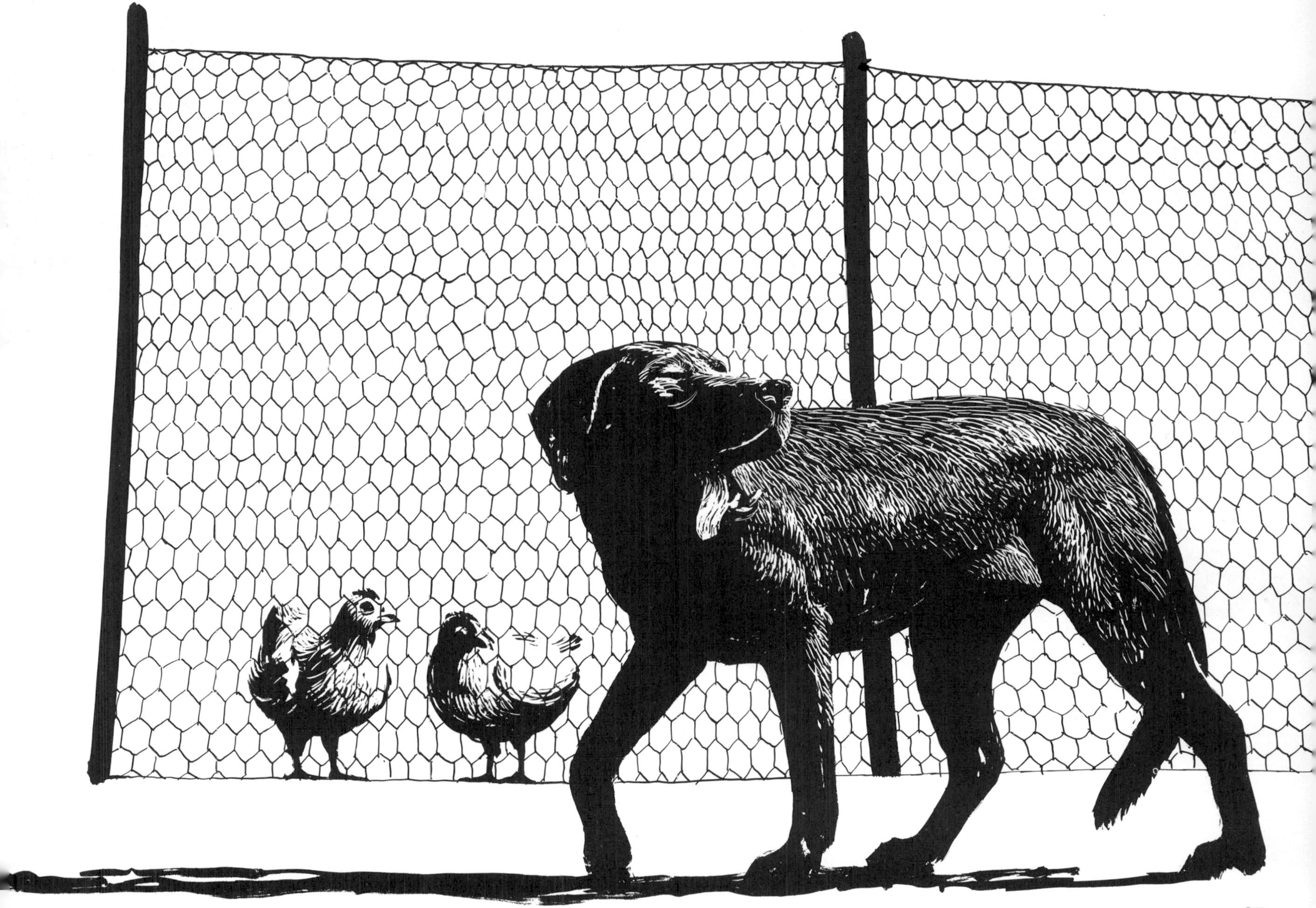

In the days that followed, the land was reseeded; and in the months that followed, wild rye grass grew again, and white clover blossomed in patches and covered the black earth.

At the edge of the forest, new branches showed green,

and little animals found shelter in trees and in burrows.

The fox hunted for his supper.

When he had eaten, he lay safe in his cave, and he cleaned his fur and pulled the burrs from between his toes. And then he slept.

When the moon rose low over the valley, he awakened and went outside and rolled in the cool dirt and shook himself.

He pointed his nose toward the big round moon and howled, long and mournfully.

He heard a distant bark, a warning bark.

Far down in the valley, the dog was answering his call. The fox sniffed the air, and he smelled the good, cool, damp smell of green growing things, and trotted off into the forest.